fuchsia

willow herb

violet

primrose

potentilla

poppy

rose

pansy

bluebell

milkweed seed

pansy

tulip

viola

acorn

wild geranium

pansy

primrose

geranium

maple seed

wild hyacinth

cosmos

Tricycle Press
a little division of Ten Speed Press
P.O. Box 7123, Berkeley, California 94707
www.tenspeed.com

Design by Jane McCampbell
Translated by Raegen Salais Fabre
Typeset in Weiss, Gando, and Monterey

Library of Congress Cataloging-in-Publication Data

Peyre, Virginie. [Grand bal des fleurs. English]
The blossoms' ball / Virginie Peyre ; Danielle Stein-Aubert. p. cm.
Summary: Over the course of one week, the flower children blossom into a variety of flowers, just in time for the grand ball.
ISBN 1-58246-096-5 [1. Flowers—Fiction. 2. Fairies—Fiction.] I. Stein-Aubert, Danielle.
II. Title. PZ7.P44819 Bl 2003
[E]—dc21 2002009179

First printing, 2003. Printed in China.
1 2 3 4 5 6 — 07 06 05 04 03

The Blossoms' Ball

by Danielle Stein-Aubert

Illustrations by Virginie Peyre

TRICYCLE PRESS

Berkeley   Toronto

The day fairy tiptoes into the garden and lifts the sheets of mist. The morning elves greet the flower children.

"A gentle breeze to brush Primrose's hair," whispers the day fairy.
"A kiss of light to waken Buttercup.
A drop of dew to tickle Violet.
A tender cuddle for Cosmos."

6

"For breakfast we shall have cheerfulness and good spirits," announces the day fairy. "And as much morning dew as you can drink!

Children, I have good news for you. Last night the garden elf announced that we shall have a grand ball next Sunday. Quickly, my little buds, you have only one week to blossom into flowers!"

Drawing lessons are the order of the day at the School of Flowers. Miss Rose gives everyone a large sheet of paper.

"A blossom's life begins with its leaves. Leaves can be simple or complicated. Picture in your mind the leaf you want, draw it on your sheet of paper, and then clip it out with your scissors. No copycats!"

Buttercup snoozes and dreams that his leaves grow and grow.

8

The children think,
and imagine,
and draw,
and snip
away at their pictures.

Lily of the Valley, usually so merry,
is grumpy this morning. "I don't know how to
draw. I like to sing. When I grow up, I want
to be a musician!"

9

Tuesday

1. The sil - ver rain - drops pat - ter up - on the earth to -
2. "Tap, tap," their knock is gen - tle, and this is what they

day.

say:

1. O lit - tle flow - ers
2. Come out in pret - ty

wa - ken and o - pen wide your door.
dress - es for spring it comes once more.

The sunbeams play with the morning mist. Cosmos is out of sorts. He wants to play, too.

"Everyone take your places for the
dance lesson!"

Miss Rose hums the melody and
little feet jump about.

Pirouette, chassé, plié.
Music fills the flower children with joy.

"Dance my little ones, graceful and light as ribbons.

Now take your bows and curtsy."

12

Prance...

Dance...

Give your partner a playful glance.

Come, join us.

See us dance!

13

Lace of dew and veils of mist,
threads of silver and yards of silk,
golden buttons—the School of Flowers
has become a busy workshop.

14

"My, you are all growing so quickly," says Miss Rose.
"This morning we shall have a sewing lesson. Design
your costume for
Sunday's ball and
trim the fabric. Don't
forget the accessories:
dewdrop necklaces,
satin ribbons, pollen hats,
cobweb stockings, and
mossy slippers."

"My dress is too long!"
"My veil is all torn!"

Miss Rose has nimble fingers.

15

"Let your inspiration guide you," says Miss Rose.

"Try something different. Have fun!"

"I will be the most beautiful flower," thinks proud Daisy. "There will be as many petals on my dress as there are pearls on my crown."

Hidden in a far-off corner of the garden, Buttercup frowns in concentration as he embroiders his golden garlands. Nearby, Cosmos daydreams.

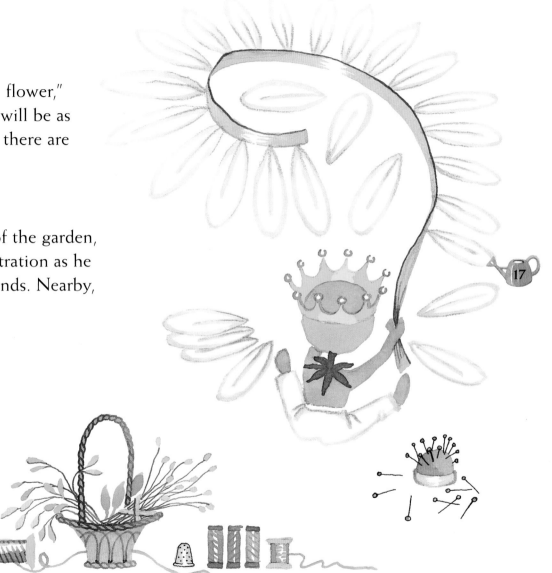

It's Thursday! Yippee!" shouts Poppy.
Painting lessons, color lessons. So much to learn!

"This morning, we will explore. This afternoon, we will finish our painting," says Miss Rose. "Let us open our eyes to the world. Colorful objects are all around us and they will help us choose the best colors for our petals."

"Who would like to be sunbeam yellow?"
"I would, I would!" says Primrose.

18

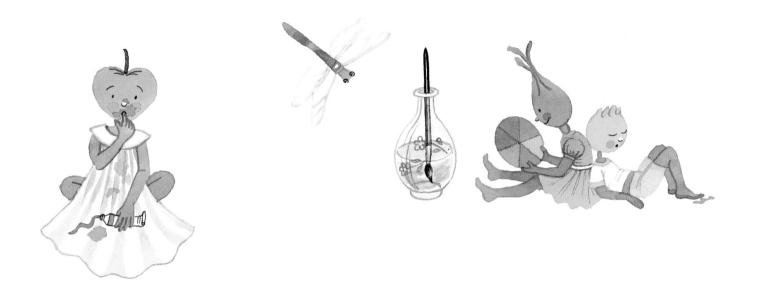

"I want a dress like yours," whispers Bleeding Heart to Miss Rose.

"If you mix a little white with your red, you'll get a pink just like mine," answers her teacher.

Ladylike Tulip carefully colors the bodice of her dress.

"Remember, choosing your colors is an important decision. They must be bright and bold and look wonderful together if we want the butterflies to visit us."

"Who wants strawberry red?"
"I do!" says Poppy.

From the tips of the flower children's brushes or the tips of their fingers, colors of butterfly wings and sweet things make their way to the costumes.

Cosmos is still mixing colors. "If you add this pink to this blue," Miss Rose gently whispers in his ear, "you'll get the color you're looking for."

"When we've finished, we will wash our hands and have some milk and cookies."

"Hurray!" cries out Primrose.

Friday morning, enormous rain clouds hover over the garden. Lightning tears the sky.

The Wind whistles furiously,
unraveling Anemone's hat, toppling Tulip,
and scattering Violet's petals.

The flower children shiver
as the storm rumbles and crashes.

22

Large drops beat down on the fragile leaves.
Rain drenches the delicate silk dresses.
The flower children feel lost and sad.

But soon sunlight floods the garden.
"Dry your tears," says the Sun. "Thanks to the rain,
tomorrow you will have grown and
everything will be as it should."

23

And so, the night unfolds
its veil of dreams.

Shhhh…

The garden elf works quietly through the night. From his secret hiding place he brings out flasks and bottles, boxes and bundles.

"Some gold dust for Buttercup. Tinkling bells for Lily of the Valley. Scarlet ribbons for Tulip and a pistil hat for Anemone.

Velvet leaves for Violet and Primrose, and fresh dirt for Daisy. And lots of shiny leaves for Wild Rose."

25

On Saturday morning, rays of sunlight brighten the garden. From the warm, damp earth, Miss Rose picks the right scent for each blossom child. Mother Lily of the Valley has come to help for the day.

"We shall need a dainty scent, I think, for White Lilac," she says.
"And a sweet scent for Daisy. A musky scent for Wild Rose.
An exotic scent for Violet. A delicate scent for Buttercup.
And a spicy scent for Cosmos."

"The dance is tomorrow, children," says Miss Rose.
"Iron your party clothes, brush off your shoes,
and practice your steps."

"Bravo, Poppy. Your hat is a great success!"

"May I polish my thorns?" asks Wild Rose.

26

The day of the grand ball is here at last. When the Sun unfolds the petals on the blossoms, he is surprised by their sparkling, rainbow-colored costumes.

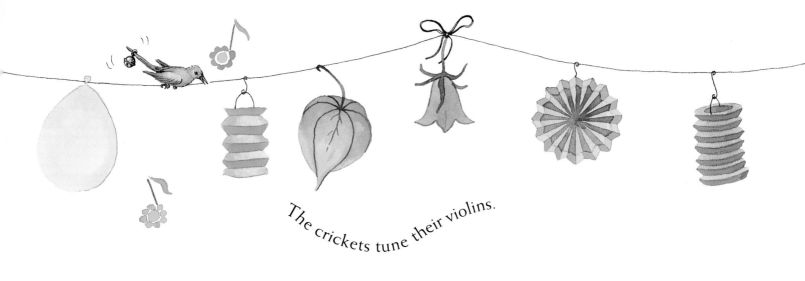

The crickets tune their violins.

The nightingale practices its trills.

The cicadas chirp their sweet song.

29

On the scented velvet
of the spring moss,
the dance begins.
The music echoes
in the hearts of
the flower
children.

30

"We are grown now," says Tulip.

"What fun we shall have!"

31

The
End

Class Photograph of the School of Flowers

fuchsia

willow herb

violet

primrose

potentilla

poppy

rose

pansy

bluebell

pansy

milkweed
seed

tulip

viola

wild geranium

acorn

pansy

primrose

geranium

maple seed

wild hyacinth

cosmos